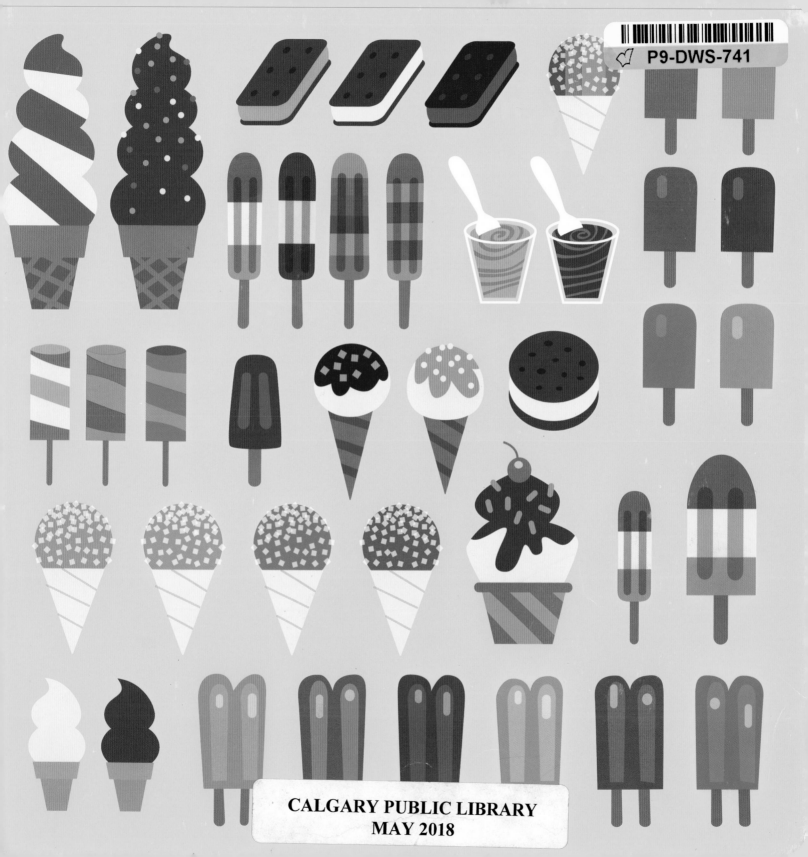

For Harold Grinspoon
—M. C.

For Jonathan & Heather
—B. K.

Henry Holt and Company, *Publishers since 1866*
Henry Holt® is a registered trademark of Macmillan Publishing Group, LLC
175 Fifth Avenue, New York, NY 10010
mackids.com

Text copyright © 2018 by Margery Cuyler
Illustrations copyright © 2018 by Bob Kolar

Library of Congress Cataloging-in-Publication Data is available.
ISBN 978-1-62779-806-8

Our books may be purchased in bulk for promotional, educational, or
business use. Please contact your local bookseller or the Macmillan Corporate
and Premium Sales Department at (800) 221-7945 ext. 5442 or by e-mail at
MacmillanSpecialMarkets@macmillan.com.

First edition, 2018
The artist used Adobe Illustrator on a Macintosh computer to
create the illustrations for this book.

Printed in China by RR Donnelley Asia Printing Solutions Ltd.,
Dongguan City, Guangdong Province
1 3 5 7 9 10 8 6 4 2

The Little Ice Cream Truck

Margery Cuyler

illustrated by Bob Kolar

Christy Ottaviano Books

Henry Holt and Company • New York

I'm a little ice cream truck,
my driver's name is Lou.
Ding-a-ling, ding-a-ling,
we're headed to the zoo.

I'm a little ice cream truck,
Lou plays a jingly tune.
"Pop! Goes the Weasel!"
I see a red balloon.

I'm a little ice cream truck,
Lou drives me to the park.
Boys and girls come running,
the dogs begin to bark.

I'm a little ice cream truck,
the kids start lining up,
smiling, leaping, shouting,
"Vanilla in a cup!"

I'm a little ice cream truck
with signs on front and rear:
CAUTION! CHILDREN CROSSING!
LOOK BOTH WAYS! STAY CLEAR!

I'm a little ice cream truck,
Rose gets a Berry Crunch.
Bob buys a lemon ice,
José a Cookie Munch.

I'm a little ice cream truck,
we have so many treats:
milkshakes, cones, and Bomb Pops,
Fudgsicles, ices, sweets.

I'm a little ice cream truck,
I'm rented for events—
celebrations, birthdays,
big parties under tents.

I'm a little ice cream truck,
we're off to Lilac Lane.
Happy birthday, Tony!
Let's hope it doesn't rain.

I'm a little ice cream truck,
the guests are having fun,
licking, laughing, singing.
Tony's turning one!

I'm a little ice cream truck,
we watch a baseball game.
The players take a break,
excited that we came.

I'm a little ice cream truck,
it's just another day.
I make the children happy,
I love my job—hooray!